AF575908

Major League SOCCER

San Jose Earthquakes

QUAKES
SAN JOSE 1974

John Bankston

Printing 1 2 3 4 5 6 7 8

First Edition, 2020.
Author: John Bankston
Designer: Ed Morgan
Editor: Lisa Petrillo

Series: Major League Soccer
Title: San Jose Earthquakes / by John Bankston

Hallandale, FL : Mitchell Lane Publishers, [2020]

Library bound ISBN: 9781680204926
eBook ISBN: 9781680204933

PHOTO CREDITS: Design Elements, freepik.com, newscom.com, APImages, p. 14 Ryan Knapp CC-BY-SA-2.0, Getty Images

Contents

Words in **bold** throughout can be found in the Glossary.

Soccer Valley

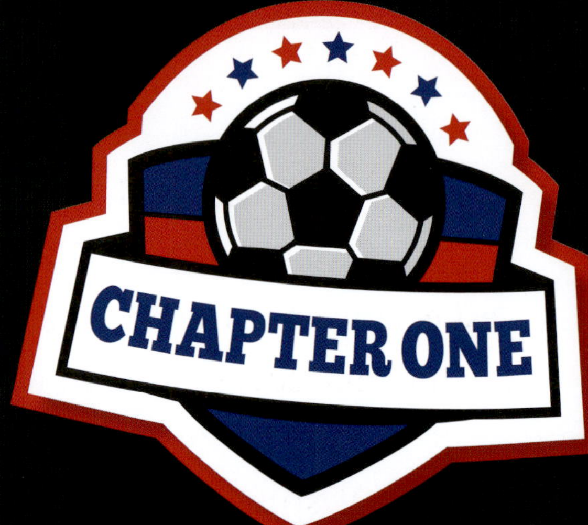

Do you have a smartphone? Do you watch videos on a tablet or write letters and reports on a computer? Much of the **technology** powering those handy devices was invented in San Jose, California. The city isn't just a tech pioneer. It's a soccer pioneer, too. In 1996, the first goal in a new **professional** league was scored in San Jose.

The city is part of Santa Clara County in Northern California near San Francisco. Almost 50 years ago, journalist Don C. Hoefler called it "Silicon Valley." The well-known writer named it after a chemical used in making the electronic circuits running computers. Computer inventions helped make San Jose important in the world. So did soccer.

Soccer is the most played game in the world! It is often called "football." That's because players use their feet to move the ball. The word "soccer" came from England. This is also where we get today's soccer rules.

California was settled by Spain, England, Mexico, and Portugal starting in the 1500s. It was filled with a mix of cultures, especially after the famous discovery of gold in 1848. In Northern California, soccer arrived with **immigrants** from Mexico and Portugal. By the early 1900s, amateur soccer leagues had started like the Pastimes and Vampires Football Club. San Jose State University fielded its first college team in the 1920s.

Lots of people played soccer. Few paid to watch it.

Chapter One

In the 1960s, the North American Soccer League (NASL) was one of the first professional leagues in the U.S. In 1974, it added teams. Teams were started in Vancouver, Canada, Seattle, Washington, and Los Angeles, California. The fourth West Coast team almost went to San Francisco. Instead, an immigrant named Milan Mandric who earned his fortune selling electronics bought a pro team for San Jose. Mandric loved soccer and wanted his team playing in his adopted hometown. The local newspaper sponsored a contest for readers to name their team. Readers voted to call them the Earthquakes.

"In the early 1970s, there was nothing to do here," author Gary Singh explained to a reporter. "There had never been anything like professional sports in our city." San Jose soccer fans really supported the Earthquakes, nicknaming them the "Quakes." Attendance at home games was often higher than in larger NASL cities.

The Earthquakes never won a championship. One highpoint came in 1975 when the team won an indoor **tournament** against the Tampa Bay Rowdies. The NASL **folded** in 1984. San Jose's team still had many fans. The Earthquakes joined the Western Soccer League. The team lasted four more years. Long before the Quakes stopped playing, most fans stopped watching.

In Northern California, other pro sports teams are successful in San Francisco and Oakland. Football fans cheer on the '49ers and loved the Oakland Raiders. Baseball fans support the Oakland Athletics and the San Francisco Giants. These teams have some of the best players in the sport. In soccer, the best players around the world compete in the World Cup. Different countries host the tournament every four years. Soccer fans travel long distances to cheer on their favorite teams.

The United States team did not do well in the World Cup before the 1990s. The country still wanted to host the highly popular tournament. To do this, the U.S. needed to create a professional soccer league. Major League Soccer (MLS) was born.

In 1994, more people attended U.S.-hosted World Cup matches than ever before. In Northern California, more than 500,000 people attended quarterfinal matches at Stanford University's **stadium**.

Fans packed the stands during MLS's opening season in 1996. Soccer fans were thrilled to finally have a professional soccer league in the U.S.

Two years later, MLS began. There were just 10 teams. San Jose was one of them. At first, the League struggled. In 2002, the U.S. reached the World Cup quarterfinals for the first time. More people became fans. They started watching MLS games.

"Professional soccer, I believe, is here to stay in the United States," former D.C. United coach, Bruce Arena, told *The Chicago Tribune* newspaper in 2005. "The existence and growth of MLS has developed a dream for young kids." By 2018, the average MLS game drew more than 20,000 fans per game.

Today there are 24 teams in the MLS. Twenty-one of those play in U.S. cities. Three more play in Canada. In 2020, new teams will play in Miami, Florida, and Nashville, Tennessee.

Teams compete in two divisions, the Eastern and Western. San Jose plays in the Western. Like the other clubs, San Jose plays 17 games at home, and 17 away games. Regular season play runs from March until October.

When a team wins, it gets three points. A tie gives a team one point. There are no points for losses. At the end of the season, the dozen top teams go to the playoffs. Six teams from the Western Conference compete, and six from the Eastern Conference. The two teams that win the most conference games compete for the MLS Championship in December.

When San Jose began playing in the MLS, a sneaker company owned part of the League. The company didn't want a soccer team carrying their name in case it failed. So the San Jose team was called The Clash. Fans soon decided the new name was a curse. They believed the biggest disaster was the team's losing record.

Fun Facts

1. **In 2026, North America hosts the World Cup. Just 20 of the 80 games will be played outside of the United States—in Canada and Mexico.**
2. **The Earthquakes play home games in black uniforms with blue and black stripes. Their away colors are white with blue lines along the edge of the uniform.**

Earthquakes 2.0

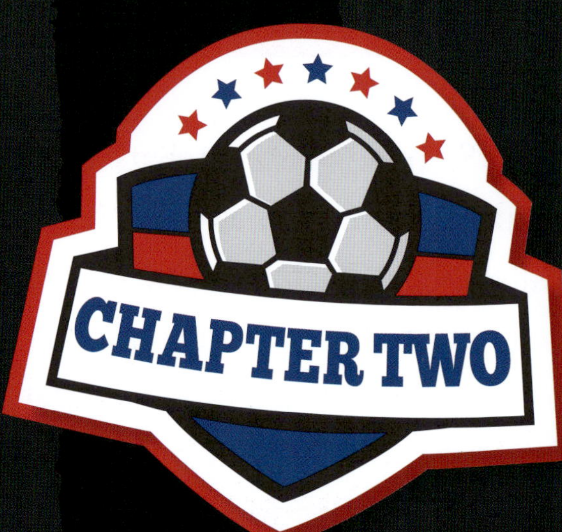

The very first Major League Soccer game was in San Jose. The Clash's captain John Doyle was worried. "We didn't know if people were going to turn up," Doyle wrote on the team's website. He wasn't sure locals wanted to watch MLS games.

They surprised him. More than 30,000 people packed San Jose State's Spartan Stadium for that first game on April 6, 1996. The match between the Clash and D.C. United also aired on ESPN. No player scored for 87 brutal minutes. Would the first pro soccer game in the U.S. end with a 0-0 tie?

Suddenly, Clash forward Eric Wynalda shot past D.C. defender Jeff Agoos and sent the ball into the goal. The Clash had won!

The new San Jose team was linked to the old one. Clash General Manager Peter Bridgwater had owned the Earthquakes in the 1980s. "I think Peter made it easier for MLS to say 'San Jose is a good place for us.' We owe a lot to him," Doyle told a reporter.

By season's end, the Clash was No. 4 in its conference. The team made the playoffs!

At Spartan Stadium, San Jose's players faced their Southern California **rivals**. The L.A. Galaxy had beaten the Clash in every regular season match. The Clash won the first semifinal with a single goal. At Pasadena's Rose Bowl stadium, the team lost both games. The Galaxy advanced.

The 1996 season was the Clash's best. In 1997 and 1998, the teammembers ranked last in their conference. In 2000, they earned just 29 points. The team was dead last in the MLS.

Everything changed in 2001. The National Hockey League's San Jose Sharks began running the Clash. The team got its old name back. "It would have been a lot easier, I think, if we'd kept it as Earthquakes all the way through," former player Chris Dangerfield told a sportswriter.

Winning takes more than regaining a new favorite old name. When Landon Donovan joined the Earthquakes, he was barely out of high school.

San Jose Clash's Braeden Cloutier is upended by Columbus Crew's Andy Williams in the first half at Spartan Stadium in San Jose, CA, May 1999.

Chapter Two

Landon Donovan holds up the Most Valuable Player trophy after the MLS All-Star Game in July 2001.

With his bleached blond hair and easy confidence, the 19-year old Californian became the team's best-known player. From late spring until early summer, the Earthquakes won all but one game.

In July, top players competed in the MLS All-Star game. Six Earthquakes played in the 2001 game—a record number from one team. Donovan played alongside teammates Ronald Cerritos, Joe Cannon, Troy Dayak, and Manny Lagos. They were joined by former United defender Jeff Agoos. The game ended in a tie of 6-6, a high-scoring game in soccer. Donovan scored four goals and was named Most Valuable Player.

By October, the Earthquakes headed to the playoffs. The team made MLS history. They increased their combined season points from 29 in 2000 to 45 in 2001.

Yet the winning record didn't help attendance. Most home games that year drew fewer than 10,000 people, the lowest in the League.

The Earthquakes needed just two games to defeat the Columbus Crew in the quarterfinals. They faced the team with the best record in the League. Miami Fusion won the first match. At home, the Earthquakes defeated the Florida team 4-0. At Fort Lauderdale's Lockhart Stadium, the Earthquakes endured a scoreless game. During overtime, defender Jimmy Conrad sent the ball into the air. Fellow defender Troy Dayak leapt up and kicked it past the Miami goalkeeper. For the first time, the Earthquakes teammembers were headed for the championships!

To win the Cup, they would have to beat their biggest rivals, the L.A. Galaxy. The Quakes were soon down a goal against LA. Then earth shook for the Quakes as Donovan scored the tying goal in the 43rd minute of the game. Once again, San Jose players' hopes went into overtime. After just six minutes of extra time, forward Dwayne De Rosario scored the winning goal. The Earthquakes were MLS Cup Champions!

Two years later, the Earthquakes did it again. In November, the Quakes beat the Chicago Fire 4-2 to win the MLS Cup Championship game.

Winning two Cups in three years would be amazing for any MLS team. It was even sweeter for the Earthquakes. Then in 2004, joy turned to anger.

Changes were happening to the team that had worked so hard for survival. MLS officials wanted to change the team's name again, to San Jose America. The new owners also ran Mexico's Club América. Then they traded San Jose star Landon Donovan

to the rival L.A. Galaxy. The name change never happened. Instead, the team changed its hometown and state. The Earthquakes were leaving California.

At the end of the 2005 season, the team moved. In the breakup, San Jose got to keep the team colors, name and logo. The actual team, however, was renamed the Dynamo, and the remaining Quake players and coaches were replanted to Houston. San Jose no longer had an MLS team.

The main reason officials wanted to leave was because San Jose didn't have a soccer-specific stadium. Like all the early MLS teams, the team had shared its stadiums with other sports teams. Spartan Stadium, where the Quakes played, was built for college football. Today MLS wants its teams in stadiums and soccer turf best suited to soccer. More than one dozen teams enjoy soccer-specific stadiums.

Two years after losing their MLS team, San Jose got a new one. The new team would be called The Earthquakes. New team, same old name—it could get confusing. With a return to the beloved name, the Earthquakes got a familiar face. Frank Yallop, the coach that led the Quake players to their first Championship, returned. He'd been coaching for the team's rival, the L.A. Galaxy.

Frank Yallop in June 2011.

Yet the new Quakes failed to attract fans. Other MLS teams often drew more than 20,000 people in the stands. Before 2015, Earthquakes attendance didn't go over 15,000.

Some wondered if the lack of place to call their own was part of the problem. "They were a homeless team for 40 years," Gary Singh told MLS.com. "But not anymore."

In 2015, the Earthquakes finally got a stadium. Avaya Stadium cost $100 million to build. It used 3,174 tons of steel. And it had 18,000 seats for soccer fans.

Fans and townspeople reacted with approval to finally having a stadium best suited to soccer. More than 6,000 people came to the ceremony breaking ground for construction. It was such a huge crowd, it set a world record for a groundbreaking ceremony. Still, to win another Cup the Earthquakes, needed more than a new stadium and the best grass. They needed a coach to motivate players who excelled at the game.

Fun Facts

1 **1974 is the year the Earthquakes entered professional soccer. That date is proudly displayed on the team badges in red.**

2 **Over the past 20 years, the Earthquakes have played in six stadiums in San Jose, Palo Alto, and Oakland.**

Earthquakes Shake up the Game

The Earthquakes were in trouble. Building a winning team takes years. Coach Frank Yallop only had days. From 1998 to 2000, three different coaches failed to lead the team to the playoffs. In the past, Yallop had coached the team to the playoffs three years in a row. He did it by **drafting** top players for each position. He brought players who knew how to work as a team, and understood the basics of soccer.

This time even before the MLS draft, he traded with other teams for top players. He also brought 19-year old star Landon Donovan onto the team.

Yallop helped the Earthquakes climb all the way from last place to winning the championship. In 2001 he earned the Coach of The Year Award.

One reason soccer is popular is because the basics are simple. Players don't need a lot of equipment. And the rules don't change very often.

Goalkeeper(GK)
Right back defender (RB)
Left back defender (LB)
Center back defender (CB)
Left midfielder (LM)
Center midfielder (CM)
Right midfielder (RM)
Left forward (LF)
Right forward (RF)

Each side has 11 players. Usually the goalkeepers wear a different color. That helps the referee know who is tending the goal. Goalkeepers can use their hands.

The other players start off in a 4-4-2 formation, with two rows of four players. The last two keep close to the other team's goal. These are the forwards. They are the ones who score most often.

Defenders stay near their team's goal. Their job is to protect the goal and keep the other team from scoring.

In the middle of the field are the midfielders. These four players can defend their own goal or send the ball toward the other team's goal. Since they do both jobs, it can be a tough position. The center midfielder is often the team's captain.

Every team has three substitute players. These are called in from the bench where they replace a player on the field. That player can't go back into the game.

Soccer has two halves, 45 minutes each. The clock doesn't stop during pauses in play. To make up for this, the referee adds time at the end of the half.

Chapter Three

In 2009, the Earthquakes returned to San Jose. Just like in 2001, Coach Yallop built the team around newcomers who became stars. The 'Quakes became known for winning games in the final minutes. In a 2012 match against the Galaxy, they won by scoring three goals in 18 minutes. Striker Steven Lenhart yelled, "Goonies never say die!" Fans started screaming the phrase in the final minutes of the game. That year the team set an Earthquake record. They earned 66 points and scored 72 goals during regular season play. Yet again winning the championship meant beating L.A. Galaxy. For the first time all year, the Earthquakes lost at home. The Galaxy went on to win the Cup.

For both the Galaxy and the Earthquake players, post-season is familiar. The San Jose and L.A teams have earned seven championships between them. It's one of the strongest rivalries in the MLS.

Southern and Northern California are so different and so far apart, people joke that they are separate states. The state's coastline is more than 1,000 miles long, The weather is different at each end at a place so big. People from the north like NORCAL the best. SOCAL locals think Southern California is perfect.

Los Angeles Galaxy defender Omar Gonzalez (*top*) climbs over Steven Lenhart in a 2012 game.

When it comes to soccer, in the MLS the rivalry among fans is so deep it even has a nickname, the California Clásico. Fans of the two teams, L.A. and San Jose, consider it the only true rivalry in Major League Soccer.

In 2016, fan Dan Margarit noticed L.A. fan groups outnumbering supporters of Earthquakes during a home game. "Those guys were running all around the stadium, insulting our players, heckling our regular fans," Margarit told a reporter. "That day was a turning point. It helped me make up my mind about starting a solid group, a group willing to do whatever to defend our team, our stadium." He began a fan group called the San Jose Ultras.

With a new stadium, Earthquakes fans believe they may have a chance. Avaya Stadium's roof can be opened to let in the sun. It can be closed to keep in the noise. "You look around at the other stadiums around the League—Kansas City, Portland, Houston—who have that smaller atmosphere but get good crowds, it creates a great atmosphere," Head Coach Dominic Kinnear told a reporter.

Having a loud, hometown crowd can really help a team. It could even help the Earthquakes win another cup.

Fun Fact

Since 2004, the Earthquakes team mascot is named Q. His full name is Quakesadus Mascotacus, making him sound like a proud warrior from ancient times.

The Earthquake's Best

Many kids dream of playing pro soccer. Joe Cannon made it happen. In the early 1990s, the San Francisco Bay Blackhawks often played in San Jose. "I remember as a youth player getting to play at half-time during a Blackhawks game at Spartan Stadium," Cannon told a writer. "It was such a rush to be on that field. I felt as a young kid that it was always my destiny to play in San Jose." Cannon was one of the first players **recruited** by San Jose and played seven seasons with them.

Steven Beitashour, had a similar story. "Growing up here, I was a fan of the Quakes first; then I was a ball boy on the field, so I know how passionate and supportive the fans can be," he told the media.

It can take time to become a star. Chris "Wondo" Wondolowski followed the Earthquakes to Houston. He spent 54 months watching the games from a bench. He told a sportswriter, "To be honest, I wasn't ready. Some guys get their chance at the wrong time, too early or too late." Instead, he returned to San Jose, where Yallop was always willing to take a chance on untested players.

During more than 20 seasons, the Earthquakes have had many top players.

Chris "Wondo" Wondolowski **Forward**

Born in Danville, California (2005, 2009-2018)

Wondolowski followed the "original" Earthquakes as they moved to Houston and were renamed the Dynamo. He returned to San Jose to play for the new Earthquakes in 2009. After five seasons as a reserve player, in 2010 he scored 18 goals and earned an "MLS Golden Boot." On August 19, 2017 Wondolowski became the first player in MLS history to score ten or more goals in eight consecutive seasons. By the end of the next season, he was the second all-time leading goal scorer in MLS history.

Chris Wondolowski (*top left*) defends against Seattle Sounder Gustav Svensson on a corner kick in October 2018.

Chapter Four

Joe Cannon dives for the ball in a game against the New England Revolution in May 2008.

Joe Cannon Goalkeeper
Born in Sun Valley, Idaho (1998–2002; 2008–2010)

During his first four seasons with San Jose, he played on the 2001 Championship team and joined the MLS All-Star team in 2001 and 2002. He was also MLS Goalkeeper of the Year in 2002 and 2004. He holds the team record with 171 games played in goal. In 2000, he was named the Defensive Player of the Year. After playing for the Colorado Rapids and the L.A. Galaxy, he returned to San Jose in 2008.

Steven Beitashour Defender/Right Fullback
Born in San Jose, California (2010–2013)

Unnoticed at first, this hometown talent was named an MLS All-Star in 2012. That year he also helped the Earthquakes win the Supporters' Shield.

Landon Donovan Midfielder
Born in Ontario, California (2001-2005)
Before leaving for arch rivals L.A. Galaxy, Donovan helped lead the Earthquakes to two championships. He has scored more goals than any other player in MLS history.

Dwayne De Rosario Attacking Midfielder
Born in Ontario, Canada (2001-2005)
Although Rosario was on the Earthquakes Championship team, he only became a midfielder after Landon Donovan left to play for the Galaxy. In 2005, he won "MLS Goal of the Year." He was the only player to win two years in a row. He was also listed as MLS Best XI six times.

Florian Jungwirth Defensive Midfielder
Born in Grafelfing, Germany (2017-2018)
His first year with the Earthquakes, he was nominated for Landon Donovan MVP Award, the MLS Defender of the Year Award and the MLS Newcomer of the Year Award. His talent for protecting the goal is one reason he won the Earthquakes Defensive Player of the Year Award in 2017. Off the field he is known for his work saving dogs and speaking out against countries that harm them.

Fatai Alashe Midfielder
Born in Southfield, Michigan (2015-2018)
A talented player, he is best known for being the first to score a goal in San Jose's Avaya Stadium, helping the Earthquakes defeat the Chicago Fire 2-1.

Communication in San Jose

The top-scorer in the MLS was born in California. So was the runner-up. When players Landon Donovan and Chris Wondolowski joined the Earthquakes, they **communicated** with players from all over the world. Every team can have up to eight international players. Once those athletes came mainly from Europe. Today, leading soccer players usually arrive from South and Central America to play on the professional U.S. league.

California is already home to large numbers of people from south of the U.S.-Mexico border. Soccer is a big part of their life. In L.A., Club Deportivo Chivas USA is run by the popular Mexican team, Chivas Guadalajara. The second Los Angeles MLS team was added to reach Mexican-American fans who did not already support the League.

Sometimes players join a sports team in the middle of the season. This is hard. It's a lot like changing schools mid-year. It's even harder when you speak a different language.

Anibal Godoy (*left*) and Seattle Sounders Cristian Roldan battle for a header in October 2018.

In 2015, Dominic Kinnear became the Earthquakes new head coach. He'd coached the Dynamos when the team first moved to Houston. Before that, he was an assistant coach under Frank Yallop. The team was struggling. By August, they had played six matches and earned just one point. Kinnear recruited Anibal Godoy. The midfielder played his first match the day he arrived. The Earthquakes won the next four matches. The San Jose players beat top teams Sporting KC, D.C. United and the L.A. Galaxy. The Quakes defense was so strong, none of the opposing teams scored a single goal.

Godoy explained the challenge of being a newcomer to a reporter, saying in his native Spanish, "When I first got here I didn't know anyone. It was difficult to communicate because of the language barrier. But after time, confidence grows with your teammates, and that transfers onto the field."

Chapter Five

Sometimes it isn't the players who need help. Sometimes it's the coaches. Ramiro Corrales began his pro career as the youngest player in the MLS. After playing for North Salinas High School in Northern California, he joined the Clash in 1996. He returned to the San Jose team two different times. He also played for other MLS teams and in Norway. But his talent and experience were not the only reason Yallop made him a captain. "I obviously go to him a lot of times to ask how the boys are feeling," Yallop told a reporter in 2010. "We have a few Spanish-speaking players as well, and the language barrier is not easy to break when you're playing. My Spanish and Portuguese are nothing, and their English is limited. [Corrales] speaks both, so he speaks for everybody."

Having a player who speaks more than one language helps bond the team because all teammates are being heard. The 2019 team had its California players plus athletes born in the North, East, and South (New Hampshire, Texas, and Georgia) among other states. With such a mix of U.S. and international players, teammates try to learn each other's language. English-speaking players and coaches are learning that when a player *pase a la red*, he has passed to the net—sending the ball to the goal. When a player dives toward the ball it is *clavado*. Everyone's favorite word, "goal," is the same in both languages.

In 2017, for the first time in five years, the Quakes reached the playoffs.

The players lost in Vancouver to the Whitecaps FC 5–0 in the October 25 playoff game. Team officials decided they were ready to make changes. They hired a new head coach from Sweden, Mikael Stahre. Coach Stahre changed many things and put the Quakes into unusual lineups. On the field, the team sometimes used a 4-2-2-2. Their goal? Getting goals. The Earthquakes used the lineup to clear space so players could attack through the middle of the field. They became known for taking long shots and taking them more often than other teams. Unfortunately, the new style did not help their results. The team won just four matches all season. The San Jose Earthquakes finished the year in last place. The new coach was fired.

The Earthquakes have survived many challenges. They have been around much longer than recent Cup champs. Fans believe the team they love will once again win a championship.

Fun Fact

In the 2018 season, there were 86 MLS players from South America, 117 from Europe, 48 from Africa, and 9 from Asia and Australia. There were 377 from North America, including 290 from the United States.

What You Should Know

- Soccer is the world's most popular game. Almost 250 million people play the sport.
- A soccer-like game was used to train Chinese soldiers 2,000 years ago.
- Greeks and Romans also played a sport like soccer.
- The modern-style soccer game probably started in England some 1,800 years ago. It celebrated a victory in battle over invaders from Rome.
- In 1314, King Edward II of England declared soccer illegal.
- The name soccer came from England.
- Most people in the world call the sport football except in the United States, Canada, Japan, Korea, and Southeast Asia.
- The San Jose Earthquakes began in 1974 as one of the teams in the North American Soccer League (NASL).
- The MLS team began as The Clash.
- In 2001, they became the Earthquakes.

Quick Stats

1996 First year of play
2001, 2003 MLS Championship Cup
2005, 2012 Supporters' Shield
2002, 2003 Supporters' Shield Runners-up

San Jose Soccer Timeline

1777 San Jose, California, becomes the first city founded in the Californias, known as the Pueblo de San José de Guadalupe.

1821 San Jose becomes part of Mexico.

1848 The town becomes part of the United States.

1800s Soccer is played by many of the new immigrants to California.

1900s Amateur soccer leagues across Northern California become popular.

1920s Colleges field soccer teams including San Jose State.

1974 Playing as a team in the professional North American Soccer League, the San Jose Earthquakes play until 1984.

1985 The Earthquakes join the Western Soccer League.

1996 The first year of Major League Soccer includes the San Jose Clash.

1999 The Clash changes its name to the Earthquakes.

2001-2003 The Earthquakes reach the playoffs three seasons in a row, and win the Cup in 2001 and 2003.

2004 Quakes players and coaches move to Texas, where the team is renamed the Dynamo.

2009 The San Jose Earthquakes begin playing again in the MLS as an **expansion** team.

2018 The Earthquakes are the last place team in the MLS.

Glossary

communicate
Share information or ideas with others

draft
Choose someone to play on a sports team

expansion
In sports, an expansion team is one added to a league's original line-up

folded
In soccer, it's when a team stops playing forever

immigrants
People living in one country who were born in another

international
Players who come from other countries

professional
Performing a job for money

recruiting
Getting someone to play for your team

rival
Team competing with another for the same goal

stadium
A large arena for sports like soccer

technology
Machines built based upon science and research

tournament
A competition with contests between many teams until one team is the final winner

Further Reading

Crisfield, Deborah. *The Everything Kids Soccer Book*. Simon and Schuster. 2013.

Lock, Deborah. *Soccer School*, DK Publishing. 2015.

Killion, Ann. *Champions of Men's Soccer.* Philomel Books: 2018.

Nagelhout, Ryan. *Soccer: Who Does What?* Gareth Stevens Publishing, 2018.

Wahl, Grant. *Masters of Modern Soccer Crown.* 2018.

Woods, Mark. *Goal! Soccer Facts and Stats.* Gareth Stevens. 2011.

On the Internet

Beginners Guide to Soccer. U.S. National Soccer Team Players.
https://ussoccerplayers.com/beginners-guide-to-soccer

Players:
https://www.sjearthquakes.com/players
"Soccer Positions," ducksters.com http://www.ducksters.com/sports/soccer/positions.php

Team Website:
https://www.sjearthquakes.com

Index

About the Author

During my time in Portland, Oregon, I knew when the Timbers had a home game. Along the city's West Side, those 17 games created a parade. Fans gathered at restaurants. They crossed Burnside Boulevard in large groups, heading toward the stadium. And everywhere members of the Timbers Army chanted and cheered. In 2014, the World Cup motivated some restaurants to set up tables and giant TV screens in parking lots. Fans arrived sporting the colors of just about every team that qualified. This is what I love about soccer. It's what I love about all sports. Sure, I enjoy watching the last minute, game-saving goal. I like profiling athletes and how they handle both failure and success. But for me the most interesting part of a game is how fans and teams relate to one another. The way fans are honored, even celebrated in soccer seems to be unique in sports. Having written a biography of Apple Computer creator Steve Jobs, I was curious to learn about Silicon Valley's own soccer team, the San Jose Earthquakes. —John Bankston